Rookie of the Year... Jackie R
Gains Award on Basis of All-Round Ability

He's 'Ebony Ty Cobb' on Base Paths

First Baseman Also Rates High on Defensive Play, Hitting, Team Value

By J. G. TAYLOR SPINK
ST. LOUIS, Mo.

In selecting the outstanding rookie of 1947, THE SPORTING NEWS sifted and weighed only stark baseball values.

That Jack Roosevelt Robinson might have had more obstacles than his first-year competitors, and that he perhaps had a harder fight to gain even major league recognition, was no concern of this publication. The sociological experiment that Robinson represented, the trail-blazing that he did, the barriers he broke down, did not enter into the decision. He was rated and examined solely as a freshman player in the big leagues—on the basis of his hitting, his running, his defensive play, his team value.

Robinson had it all, and compared to the many other fine first-year men that 1947 produced, he was spectacularly outstanding.

Dixie Walker summed it up in a few words the other day when he said: "No other ball player on this club, with the possible exception of Bruce Edwards, has done more to put the Dodgers up in the race than Robinson has. He is everything that Branch Rickey said he was when he came up from Montreal.

Plunks in Ribs Result in Runs

Robinson has been a National League eye-popper this year because he has run the bases like an Ebony Ty Cobb. Carrying

Jackie All The Way

Illustrating Jackie Robinson's speed and alertness on the bases, the Dodger first baseman went all the way from first to home on a bunt in a June game against the Cubs in Chicago.

Jackie broke from first base as Gene Hermanski bunted. He dusted past second base as the pitcher threw out Hermanski at first and when he saw Stan Hack had been drawn in off third base, he sailed for the hot corner. The resulting hurried throw, confusion and lack of coverage at third gave Robinson the chance to scoot for the plate, which he crossed safely.

more than 100 runs around the bases to the plate on the punch of Reiser, Walker, Vaughan and Edwards, who followed him, Jackie has been unique as much because of his audacity as because of color. It should be emphasized that when Robinson sprinted to second base on a base on balls in Chicago, the score was 1 to 1 in the ninth inning. His daring turned into the run that broke up a vital game in the Dodgers' favor.

When Robinson galloped over home plate on a clean steal during Fritz Ostermueller's windup one night in Pittsburgh, there was no showboat aspect to the feat, there was nothing superfluous about the run; it broke a 2 to 2 tie; he scored the big run.

Enemy pitchers have plunked Robinson in the ribs more often than any

Ranks Class

JACKIE ROBINSON

JACKIE CROSSING PLATE ON HIS FIRST MAJOR LEAGUE HOME RUN, APRIL 18, AGAINST GIANTS

Brooklyn's 1947 play. Bill Roeder wrote it when he typed: "The Dodgers hit short and run long." Even such an astute baseball engineer as Branch Rickey, who visioned Robinson's place in the Dodger picture as long as 18 months ago, doubted for a long time that Robbie would find himself in 1947 and shift into high gear this season.

Naturally timid at first, more so than usual because of the pressure, the riding and the criticism to which he was subjected, the first time the Brooklyn club went to Cincinnati Robinson was hitting under .250. One of the papers ran a story that Robinson would have been benched weeks ago if he were a white man."

Enthralled The Mahatma

Many big leaguers had taken a quick squint at the Negro boy and said, "He won't do. Not good enough for the big leagues." There were untrue stories that the other Dodgers shunned Jack, that he was getting spiked in the field, plunked at the plate. All this was enough to keep an ordinary youngster subdued, well within his shell.

Rickey kept telling him to be venturesome. "Take that extra base every

as Big League Freshman

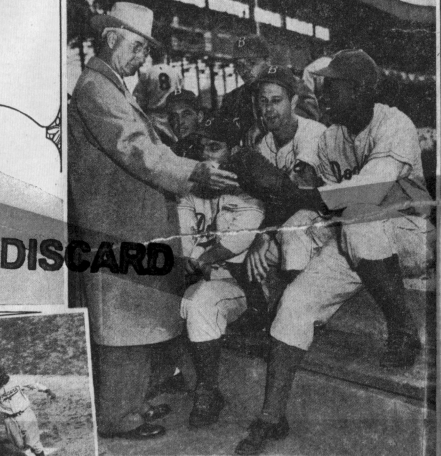

ROBINSON WITH MANAGER BURT SHOTTON AND GROUP OF TEAMMATES....

DISCARD

REACHING FOR A HIGH ONE...

Robinson's Aptitude at New Position Wins Praise from N. L. Managers

By FRED DOWN
Of the New York Sun

NEW YORK, N. Y.—"The most improved ball player of the year," is the consensus of National League managers when the subject of Jackie Robinson, the Dodgers' rookie first baseman, is discussed in the dugouts. Possibly only a player who has been called upon to cover a strange position can fully understand the difficulties which beset the former UCLA football star when he was assigned to first base in the Brooklyn infield this year.

Robinson was a second baseman in Montreal. There he had learned to make the double-play pivot, learned to move around as a second baseman should. All at once, he was a second baseman no longer. Now he was a first baseman, or so said the Brooklyn brain trust.

Robinson wasn't very good when the Dodgers returned from spring training. The Yankees expressed amazement when they saw him at first base in the three-game series between the Dodgers and Bronxites a few days before the official opening of the pennant races. They didn't believe the Dodgers could afford to go along with him.

At the time, Robinson had not acquired the felicity of glove which stamps a front-line first sacker. The experts—Bill Terry, Dolph Camilli, Joe Kuhel—handled the glove like an artist. Robinson didn't. It seemed to be getting in his way. In addition, he didn't stray much off the bag for fear that he would not be able to return in time to receive a throw to get his man. This, of course, was due to his inability to handle the glove.

All that is gone now, however. Jackie knows where and how to make all the plays. He is still not a polished first baseman but his improvement has been rapid and around the circuit every manager expresses the conviction that he will be one of the league's outstanding first basemen by the end of next year.

beaten out for hits and 28 were sacrifices. He had failed only four times. In a day when all managers are be-

My ear was glued to the radio, like every other ear in Brooklyn.

It was Opening Day, 1947. And every kid in Brooklyn knew this was our year.

The Dodgers were going to go all the way!

We had Jackie Robinson, the first Negro player in major league baseball.

As I listened to the game, the minutes melted into hours; the innings folded one into another. I could see it all in my mind's eye: pitch after pitch, swing after swing. I dreamed of the day I could see it all for myself.

Our neighborhood was only a short subway ride from Ebbets Field, home of the Dodgers and their new first baseman.

I loved baseball. I loved the Brooklyn Dodgers. I hated the New York Giants, and they hated Jackie Robinson.

One day, my father came home early from work. He walked into my bedroom and announced, "We're going to Ebbets Field."

He didn't say it out loud. My father was deaf, so he signed the words with his hands.

I couldn't believe it. Dad had never seemed to care much about baseball.

"I want to meet Jackie Robinson," Dad signed.

I was finally going to see a real game. Today the Dodgers were playing the Giants. And we were going to cream 'em.

I got my glove and ball, Dodgers cap, and scorecard. I stuck my lucky pencil behind my ear. As we went down the steps, I tossed the ball to Dad. But he'd never played baseball like me. He dropped it.

I couldn't wait to get to the ballpark. But the whole ride I kept thinking, There's no way Dad can meet Jackie Robinson. Besides, Jackie doesn't know sign language.

How would they talk to each other?

The line to get in to Ebbets Field snaked around Sullivan Place and up to Bedford Avenue. My dad let me hold my ticket. I clutched it for dear life.

Finally, we were through the turnstile. My dad held my hand as we moved with the rest of the crowd through the gloomy underbelly of the stadium, up the dark ramp. Then we tumbled into bright sunlight.

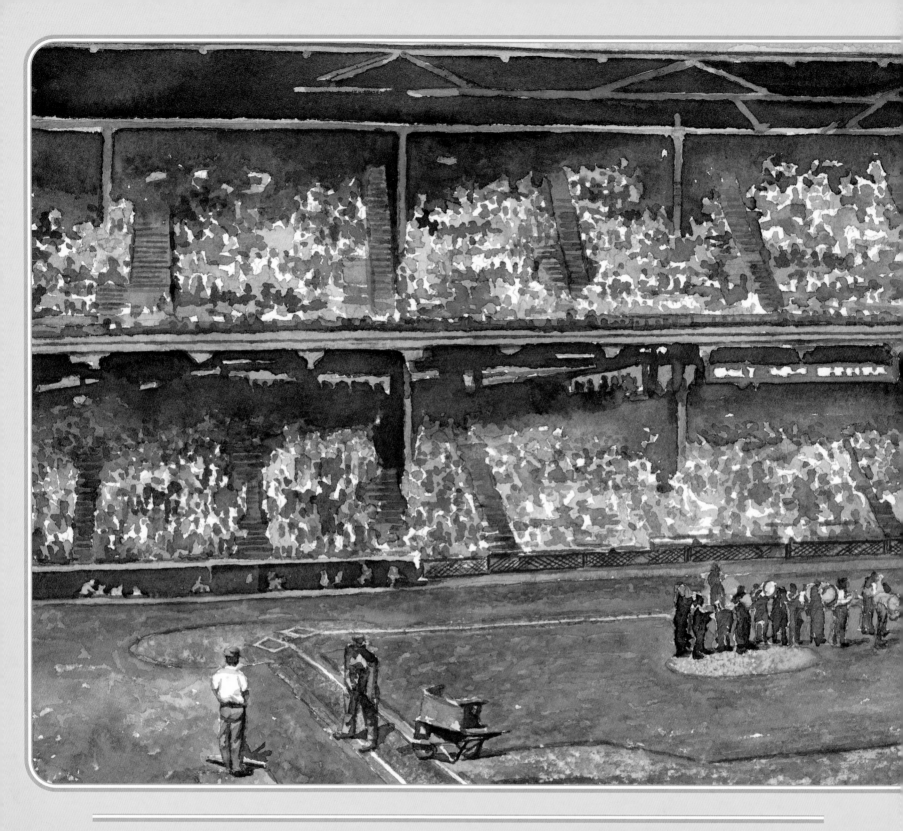

I shut my eyes against the glare. When I opened them again, my breath caught in my throat. I had never seen anything so perfect as the inside of Ebbets Field.

There, laid out at my feet, was the emerald green field, each blade of grass reflecting the light from the afternoon sun.

The angles of the field were sharply marked in two lines of white chalk.

The dirt base paths formed a perfect diamond carpet dotted with fat canvas bags at each base and a black rubber plate at home.

I knew if I lived to be a hundred, I would never again see a sight so beautiful.

"Hey, peanuts! Hey, hot dogs! Get 'em while they're hot!"

Dad and I sat on the right field line, right behind first base, Jackie's position.

The Dodgers Sym-Phony was marching up and down the aisles playing "The Worms Crawl In, the Worms Crawl Out." The music was earsplitting. Dad couldn't hear it, but he laughed along with everyone else at the sight of the raggedy band's tattered clothes, cowbells, and whistles.

When the game started and Jackie ran out on the field, Dad yelled real loud, "Jackiee, Jackiee, Jackiee!" Only it didn't come out that way. It sounded like, "AH-GHEE, AH-GHEE, AH-GHEE!" Since my dad couldn't hear, he had no way of knowing what the words should sound like.

Everyone looked at my dad.

I looked at my shoes.

As Jackie stood at first base, the Giants began hooting and hollering. They called Jackie names. Horrible names. "What are they saying?" Dad asked.

"Bad things," I said.

"Tell me." Some of those words I had to finger spell. I knew no sign for them. Dad listened with a sad little smile on his face.

In the ninth inning, Jackie bunted, and beat the throw to first. Then he stole second.

On the next Dodgers hit, he moved to third. The score was tied at four–all.

The Giants pitcher took a long windup, and Jackie dashed for home. We all jumped

to our feet yelling, "Jackiee, Jackiee, Jackiee!"

"AH-GHEE, AH-GHEE, AH-GHEE!" Dad screamed.

This time, nobody seemed to notice.

The heck with the Giants. They were nothing! We had Jackie Robinson.

Every day when Dad came home from work, he started asking me questions. Not about school. About baseball. He wanted to know everything I knew. Especially about Jackie Robinson.

"What's Jackie's batting average?"

".247," I said.

"How's that figured?"

I explained.

"What's an RBI?" he asked.

"Runs batted in."

"Fielding average. What's that mean?"

I told him.

"You teach me baseball," he signed.

"Okay," I said.

One night, Dad came home with a baseball glove.

"Let's have a catch," he signed.

We tossed the ball back and forth until Mom called us for supper. Dad missed the ball every time. The only way he could hold it was by trapping the ball against his chest with both hands. That had to hurt, but Dad just smiled.

"Jackie never drops the ball," he signed. "He catches it with one hand. Not like me."

All that week we practiced. Dad dropped the ball most every time. Even when I threw it underhand.

"Throw it regular," Dad said.

Dad and I kept going to games whenever we could. Every time Jackie came out to his position, Dad chanted right along with the crowd. AH-GHEE, AH-GHEE, AH-GHEE.

Jackie never looked over at us. He just stared down the line at the next hitter.

One Sunday, the Dodgers were playing the St. Louis Cardinals. What a game! Our pitcher had a no-hitter going.

And then it happened. On a simple grounder that he knew he couldn't beat, a Cardinal player crossed first base and spiked Jackie—on purpose! Fifty-two thousand eyes popped. Twenty-six thousand jaws dropped. Twenty-six thousand tongues were stilled.

Then, in that awful silence, my father jumped to his feet.

"NOOOO!" he screamed. "NOT FAIR! AH-GHEE, AH-GHEE, AH-GHEE!"

The Brooklyn crowd went nuts. They leapt to their feet and joined my father.

"JACK-IE, JACK-IE, JACK-IE!"

The name bounced off the brick walls, climbed the iron girders, and rattled around under the wooden roof.

But Jackie just stood at first base, his face a blank mask, blood streaming down his leg. It was almost as if he didn't hear the crowd.

All that month, Dad and I followed everything Jackie did. We read and reread every report of every game that was printed in *The New York Daily News.*

Dad started a scrapbook. If there was any mention of Jackie Robinson, he cut out the article and pasted it in his scrapbook.

The scrapbook got thicker.

The Dodgers kept winning.

And the opposing teams kept riding Jackie Robinson.

But Jackie never reacted. He didn't even seem to notice. And he never complained.

The Dodgers clinched the pennant that season when the Cards beat the Cubs.

Dad and I went downtown the next day to see the big parade to honor Jackie.

And back in the neighborhood, we had a block party to celebrate.

It didn't matter whether the Dodgers won the last game of the season, since we were already over the top. But Dad and I didn't care. We went to Ebbets Field anyway. We went to see Jackie Robinson.

In the third inning, Jackie smacked the ball to deep left field for a double. Then he flew home like the wind, his feet barely touching the base path.

The Brooklyn crowd went crazy. "Go, Go, Go, Jackieeee!"

"GOO, GOO, GOO, AH-GHEEEE!" my dad screamed right along with them.

Finally, late in the day, as deep shadows stretched across the infield, Jackie caught a line drive hit down the first base line. It was the last out of the game.

As the crowd cheered, Jackie stood alone at first base, staring at the ball in his glove.

Then he turned and threw it into the stands—right to my father!

That's when my dad did something he had never done before. He reached up and caught the ball in his bare hand!

I'm not sure, but I think I saw Jackie Robinson smile. My dad dropped the ball into my empty glove.

And just like that, the baseball season of 1947 was over.

This story is a work of fiction. Parts of it, however, are based in truth.

My father, who was deaf and spoke only with his hands, worked as a printer for *The New York Daily News*. One night in 1947, he brought home the paper—the ink not quite dry—and excitedly showed me the bold headline: BROOKLYN DODGERS SIGN JACKIE ROBINSON. Beneath it was a photo of two smiling men: the president of the Brooklyn Dodgers, Branch Rickey, and the grandson of a slave, Jackie Robinson.

"Now, at last," my father signed to me, "a Negro will play in the major leagues!"

And from the day he joined the Brooklyn Dodgers until the day he retired, Jackie Robinson was the main topic of conversation in our small Brooklyn apartment during every baseball season.

My father could not throw or catch a baseball, let alone hit one. As a boy in 1910, he attended a deaf residential school, where playing sports was not encouraged. In those days most people considered deaf children severely handicapped and thought teaching them sports a waste of time. What could my deaf father possibly have in common with this Negro baseball player, Jackie Robinson?

During Jackie's first year as a Dodger, my father took me to many games. He told me to watch carefully how the opposing team would single Jackie out for unfair treatment, how they would actively discriminate against him on the field just because his skin was brown. "Just you watch," he said. "Jackie will show them that his skin color has nothing to do with how he plays baseball. He will show them all that he is as good as they are."

Throughout his life my father also experienced the cruelty of prejudice. "It's not fair that hearing people discriminate against me just because I am deaf," he told me. "It doesn't matter, though," he always added. "I show them every day I am as good as they are."

One summer day, late in that rookie season of 1947—during which Jackie had quietly endured racial taunts, threats on his life, numerous bean balls, and even deliberate spikings—my father told me about another hero.

"There was a deaf man born in 1862," he signed to me, "who was also a baseball player. His name was William Ellsworth Hoy, but his teammates quickly nicknamed him 'The Amazing Dummy.'

"In those days no one could imagine that a deaf man could play major league baseball. The deaf were thoughtlessly called 'deaf and dumb.' It was common for the hearing to refer to a deaf person as a 'dummy.'

"But Dummy Hoy showed them all," my father continued. "He played fourteen years in the major leagues. He was smart and fast like Jackie, and in his rookie year he stole a record eighty-two bases. One day, he threw three men out at home plate from the outfield, which had never been done before. And, most importantly, he taught umpires to use hand signals to call balls and strikes."

As he told that story, I began to understand the connection between Jackie Robinson and my deaf father. Like Dummy Hoy before them, they were both men who worked to overcome thoughtless prejudice and to prove themselves every day of their lives.

—M.U.

Dedication

This book is dedicated in loving memory to Bob Domozych: Brooklyn boy, Dodger fan, Brandeis pioneer, and above all, my great, irreplaceable friend. And to my wife, Karen, with love, as always.

—*M. U.*

I dedicate this book to Brooklyn and all baseball lovers.

—*C. B.*

Acknowledgments

Special thanks to Sarah Helyar Smith, who first encouraged me to write about my deaf father and his emotional connection to the great Jackie Robinson; to Lisa Banim, whose sensitive editing helped me rethink and reshape the story; to Loraine Joyner, who transformed my words into an eye-popping book; to Margaret Quinlin, my dear steadfast friend, who was the first to give me permission to be a writer and is always ready with wise counsel; and to all the rest of the amazing Peachtree family.

I am also grateful to Francine I. Henderson, Research Administrator of the Auburn Avenue Research Library on African-American Culture and History in Atlanta, GA; the National Baseball Hall of Fame and Museum in Cooperstown, NY; and to Margot Hayward, Brooklynite and Brooklyn Dodgers fan extraordinaire, for help in authenticating the setting for this story.

Published by

Ω

Peachtree Publishers

1700 Chattahoochee Avenue   Atlanta, Georgia 30318-2112
www.peachtree-online.com

ISBN 1-56145-329-3

Text © 2005 by Myron Uhlberg
Illustrations © 2005 by Colin Bootman

Illustrations created in watercolor on Arches Aquarelle 100% rag paper. Scrapbook-page endpapers courtesy of Margot Hayward from her private collection. Text typeset in FontShop International's FF Acanthus; headings and large capitals typeset in SWFTE International's Gravure; title created with Adobe Charcoal.

Book design by Loraine M. Joyner

10 9 8 7 6 5 4 3

Printed in Singapore

Library of Congress Cataloging-in-Publication Data

Uhlberg, Myron.
   Dad, Jackie, and me / written by Myron Uhlberg ; illustrated by Colin Bootman.-- 1st ed.
      p. cm.
Summary: In Brooklyn, New York, in 1947, a boy learns about discrimination and tolerance as he and his deaf father share their enthusiasm over baseball and the Dodgers' first baseman, Jackie Robinson.
   ISBN 1-56145-329-3
   [1. Baseball--Fiction. 2. Deaf--Fiction. 3. Toleration--Fiction. 4. Robinson, Jackie, 1919-1972--Fiction. 5. Brooklyn Dodgers (Baseball team)--Fiction. 6. Brooklyn (New York, N.Y.)--History--20th century--Fiction.] I. Bootman, Colin, ill. II. Title.

PZ7.U3257Dad 2005
[Fic]--dc22
2004016711

500,000 Fans Cheer Dodgers at Flag Rally

Jackpot for Pair of Jacks

JACKIE ROBINSON, first baseman of the Dodgers, dangles his "Rookie of the Year" award before the sparkling eyes of Jackie, Jr. A Longines watch was presented to Robinson by Publisher J. G. Taylor Spink of THE SPORTING NEWS at Brooklyn's celebration honoring the Dodgers, September 26.

Crowds Hail Uniformed Flock in Victory Parade; Reception at Borough Hall Climaxes Celebration

By A. VAN PELT

BROOKLYN, N. Y.

Nearly half a million Brooklyn citizens roared a welcome to the pennant-winning Dodgers on the afternoon of September 26, with a parade and celebration that was a tumultuous mixture of pageantry and pandemonium.

It was the first time since 1941, and the fourth since the turn of the century, that the Dodgers had won a pennant and the Flatbush citizenry, from Borough President John Cashmore to babes in the arms of cheering parents, turned out to honor the team on the historic occasion. They hailed the conquering heroes with snowstorms of paper, shouts and frantic waves as the hour-long parade wound its way through jammed streets.

The tribute was the result of a suggestion by Editor Jack Lait on the editorial page of the New York Daily Mirror. Originally, it was planned to include the Yankees in a city-wide celebration, but they were unable to take part, and the ceremonies were made an exclusive Brooklyn affair.

The parade officially started at Grand Army Plaza on the fringe of Prospect Park. Seventeen automobiles carried the Dodgers, dressed in uniforms with blue windbreakers, in the motorcade which moved along the route to Borough Hall.

Dozens of hand-printed signs of encouragement were hung from the windows. But one renegade, possibly a Yankee fifth-columnist, had the effrontery to display a message which said: "Wait until the Yanks get you!"

More than 1,500 police were assigned to cover the parade route and to keep some semblance of order at Borough Hall, where the procession wound up. When the Dodgers reached the hall, they took their places under a huge banner reading: "All Brooklyn honors the Dodgers—1947 National League champions."

After the band played the National Anthem, which was sung by Joe Moran in his best Irish tenor, Borough President Cashmore was introduced by Eddie Dowden, chairman of the official reception committee. Some of the Dodger players hoisted the National League pennant to the booming of kettle drums.

Music was furnished by bands from Long Island University and Brooklyn Technical High School, as well as Shorty Laurice's "Sim-Phony" Dodger orchestra, which had accompanied the parade in a sound truck.

One by one, the borough president introduced the 27 eligible World's Series players and, with a brief tribute to each, presented to him a 21-jeweled

---

When Cookie Lost His Ginger
NEW YORK, N. Y.

Cookie Lavagetto

The big clock on the wall showed 4:57. Tiny Griffin, the 260-pound No. 1 Brooklyn Dodger rooter, watched the ashes of his cigar roll idly down his vest. Old Dan Comerford, the Brooks' property man since Sherman made his march to the sea, fumbled around with nothing, just to keep busy.

Over in the corner of the clubhouse sat the man who the day before had been the toast of Flatbush and the hero of the nation—Cookie Lavagetto. His hit, a double, in the ninth inning with two out, the Dodgers trailing, 2 to 1, and two men on bases had deprived Floyd Bevens of a no-hit game, given Brooklyn a 3 to 2 victory and put a greater-than-Hollywood climax to the most dramatic finish in the history of sport.

But this was...

Rohe, Ehmke, Passeau, etc.

We remembered other heroes—other Series. In 1906, George Rohe, an unknown, hit two triples that helped the White Sox win over the Cubs. That was a record until Bill Johnson broke it this year. Rohe remained with the Pale Hose in 1907 and then went back to the minors to stay. However, George is always remembered as the man who hit the two triples.

Home Run Baker of the Athletics never hit more than 11 circuit clouts in a season in his career. Yet he made two against Christy Mathewson and the Giants in 1911 and has been known as Home Run Baker ever since.

In 1929, Howard Ehmke fanned 13 Cubs in the first game with the Athletics. He was the toast of the baseball world. A few days later—and how many of you remember it?—he was driven out of the box. Yet he will always be remembered as the man who struck out 13 in a World's Series game.

In 1941, Mickey Owen, one of the finest catchers in baseball, dropped a third strike and the Dodgers lost the Series. Owen caught many great games after that, but the fans always remembered him as the fellow who missed the third strike on Tommy Henrich in 1941.

In 1945, Claude Passeau shut out the Tigers with one hit in the third game. He tried to come back later and was chased from the slab. But baseball fans, the toughest critics in the world, made excuses for him, remembering only his brilliant one-hit performance.

So, too, the fans have forgotten that Lavagetto struck out the next day. They only remember his greatest moment—the two-base hit which is painted on the wall of Ebbets Field as an undying shrine to the greatest climax in 44 years of World's Series play.

Born to Make Headlines

Some men are born to great moments. Cookie Lavagetto is...

Uncle Sam to Receive $150,000 Tax From Larry

WASHINGTON, D. C. — When Uncle Sam gets through with Larry MacPhail, the former head of the New York Yankees will have "only" about a million and a half left out of the $2,000,000 he received in payment for his one-third share of the club from his ex-partners, Dan Topping and Del Webb, at their split-up meeting in New York Tuesday, October 7.

According to tax experts, Uncle Sam will receive a maximum tax of $450,000 or the 25 per cent federal capital gains tax levied against the apparent profit of $1,800,000 on Larry's reported original investment of $200,000, when the colonel, Topping and Webb purchased the New York ... club for ... $2,000,000 ...

scorecard at Cookie. "Hit another one like that tomorrow."

Lavagetto signed and signed and signed some more. Finally he was free and on the way to the subway. He turned about with a puzzled but happy look. "Not a word about today, just about yesterday," he breathed. He smiled.

BILL McGOWAN

No. 1 in Service

in those days and a good one. One day my brother, Jack, was an umpire and fast ones at me, and I had a better bucket foot than Al Simmons. "My brother, Jack, was an umpire in those days and a good one. One day ... and baseman. I could field and throw, set on it," Bill recalled. "I was a second base ball player—my heart was set on it," Bill recalled. "I wanted to be the Du Pont company. "I wanted to be ...

I went to New Castle, Del. On the first few pitches I closed my eyes and guessed. I knew that would never do, so I picked up a ball, fitted it in the holes of my mask, saw that it couldn't go through and kept my eyes open from then on. Some of the boys, when they get sore, say that I still close my eyes and call 'em."

That was the beginning of McGowan's career as an umpire and his finish as a player. He was 18 years old then. McGowan wasn't a big guy—just about 135 pounds and only a boy.

Umpires in those days were supposed to be big, rough fellows who could holler and punch their way to respect. Whenever Bill asked for a job, they told him he was too young. But he was a determined cuss. He went to Tri-State League games every day with his chest protector and mask, hoping something would happen to give him a chance. One day an umpire failed to show up. They called McGowan and he went behind the bat. He did such a good job that George Graham, who was president of the league, recommended him to the president of the Virginia League.

The Virginia League president laughed when he saw Bill. "You an umpire? You'll have to show me your credentials and prove you are the fellow Graham recommended to me," he said.

McGowan got the job and a raise the ...

"Be tough," he said. "But not rough. Don't let 'em push you around, but don't go looking for fights. I have always remembered that bit of advice. Jack told me how to hold the protector, wear a mask, and how to call strikes and balls.

A Parade of Animal Poems

JUMPETY-BUMPETY HOP

Kay Chorao

Dutton Children's Books ▪ NEW YORK

ACKNOWLEDGMENTS

"Moon," from *Laughing Time: Collected Nonsense* by William Jay Smith. Copyright © 1990 by William Jay Smith. Reprinted by permission of Farrar, Straus & Giroux, Inc. "Brothers," copyright © 1978 by William Cole. First appeared in *An Arkful of Animals,* published by Houghton Mifflin Company. Reprinted by permission of Curtis Brown, Ltd., and Houghton Mifflin Company. All rights reserved. "The Old Woman," from *Appley Dapply's Nursery Rhymes* by Beatrix Potter. Copyright © 1917 by Frederick Warne & Co., London. Reprinted by permission of Frederick Warne & Co. "Mice," from *Fifty-one New Nursery Rhymes* by Rose Fyleman. Copyright © 1931, 1932 by Doubleday, a division of Bantam Doubleday Dell Publishing Group, Inc. Reprinted by permission of Doubleday, a division of Bantam Doubleday Dell Publishing Group, Inc., and The Society of Authors as the literary representative of the Estate of Rose Fyleman. "The Sea Gull," by Leroy F. Jackson. Copyright © 1996 by Rand McNally. All rights reserved. "The Prayer of the Little Ducks," from *Prayers from the Ark* by Carmen Bernos de Gasztold, translated by Rumer Godden, translation copyright © 1962, renewed 1990 by Rumer Godden. Original copyright © 1947, copyright © 1955 by Editions du Cloitre. Used by permission of Viking Penguin, a division of Penguin Books USA Inc., and Curtis Brown, Ltd., as the literary representative of the Estate of Rumer Godden. "The Duck," from *Verses from 1929 On* by Ogden Nash. Copyright © 1936 by Ogden Nash. First appeared in *The Saturday Evening Post.* Used by permission of Little, Brown and Company. "Tom's Little Dog," by Walter de la Mare. Reprinted by permission of The Literary Trustees of Walter de la Mare, and The Society of Authors as their representative. "The Rabbit," from *Under the Tree* by Elizabeth Madox Roberts. Copyright © 1922 by B. W. Huebsch, Inc., renewed 1950 by Ivor S. Roberts. Copyright © 1930 by Viking Penguin, Inc., renewed copyright © 1958 by Ivor S. Roberts. Used by permission of Viking Penguin, a division of Penguin Books USA Inc. "Grandfather Frog," by Louise Seaman Bechtel. From *Another Here and Now Story Book,* edited by Lucy Sprague Mitchell. Copyright © 1937 by E. P. Dutton, renewed

copyright © 1965 by Lucy Sprague Mitchell. Used by permission of Dutton Children's Books, a division of Penguin Books USA Inc. "The Polliwog," from *Wildwood Fables* by Arthur Guiterman, copyright © 1927 by E. P. Dutton and Company. Reprinted by permission of Louise H. Sclove. "The Little Turtle," from *The Collected Poems of Vachel Lindsay.* Copyright © 1920 by Macmillan Publishing Company, renewed 1948 by Elizabeth C. Lindsay. "The Pum Na-Na Frogs," by John Lyons. From *A Caribbean Dozen,* edited by John Agard and Grace Nichols. Copyright © 1994 by John Lyons. Reprinted by permission of Walker Books Ltd, London. Published in the U.S. by Candlewick Press, Cambridge, Massachusetts. "The Lion," by Hilaire Belloc. Reprinted by permission of the Peters Fraser & Dunlop Group Ltd. "Don't Call Alligator Long-Mouth Till You Cross River," from *Say It Again, Granny* by John Agard (Bodley Head). Reprinted by permission of Random House UK Ltd. "Mrs. Peck-Pigeon," copyright © 1951 by Eleanor Farjeon. Reprinted by permission of Harold Ober Associates Inc. and David Higham Associates. "Samuel," copyright © 1972 by Bobbi Katz. Reprinted by permission of Bobbi Katz. "Jim-Jam Pyjamas," copyright © by Gina Wilson. Reprinted by permission of Gina Wilson. "The Donkey," by Gertrude Hind. Reprinted by permission of Punch. "Oliphaunt," from *The Adventures of Tom Bombadil* by J.R.R. Tolkien. Copyright © 1962, 1990 by Unwin Hyman Ltd. Copyright © renewed 1990 by Christopher R. Tolkien, John F.R. Tolkien, and Priscilla M.A.R. Tolkien. Reprinted by permission of Houghton Mifflin Company and HarperCollins Publishers Ltd. All rights reserved. "Climbing a steep hill," by Kwaso, and "'Please don't go!' I called," by Onitsura. From *More Cricket Songs,* Japanese haiku translated by Harry Behn. Copyright © 1971 by Harry Behn. Reprinted by permission of Marian Reiner. "Firefly," by Li Po. From *A Garden of Peonies,* translated by Henry H. Hart. Copyright © 1938 by the Board of Trustees of the Leland Stanford Junior University. Copyright renewed 1966 by Henry H. Hart. Reprinted by permission of the publishers, Stanford University Press.

Library of Congress Cataloging-in-Publication Data
Jumpety-bumpety hop: a parade of animal poems/[compiled and
illustrated by] Kay Chorao.—1st ed.   p.   cm.
Includes index.
Summary: A collection of poems about animals by
English and American writers.
ISBN 0-525-45825-5
1. Animals—Juvenile poetry.   2. Children's poetry, American.
3. Children's poetry, English   [1. American poetry—Collections.
2. English poetry—collections. 3. Animals—Poetry.]   I. Chorao, Kay.
PS595.A5J86   1997   811.008'0362—dc21   97-10959   CIP   AC

Published in the United States 1997 by Dutton Children's Books,
a division of Penguin Books USA Inc.
375 Hudson Street, New York, New York 10014
Designed by Sara Reynolds
Printed in USA   First Edition
1 3 5 7 9 10 8 6 4 2

For Pam Harrison, who loves animals

TENTS

MY KITTEN

Hey, my kitten, my kitten,
    And hey, my kitten, my deary!
Such a sweet pet as this
    Was neither far nor neary.

Here we go up, up, up,
    And here we go down, down, downy;
And here we go backwards and forwards,
    And here we go round, round, roundy.

Anonymous

MOON

I have a white cat whose name is Moon;
He eats catfish from a wooden spoon,
And sleeps till five each afternoon.

Moon goes out when the moon is bright
And sycamore trees are spotted white
To sit and stare in the dead of night.

Beyond still water cries a loon,
Through mulberry leaves peers a wild baboon
And in Moon's eyes I see the moon.

William Jay Smith

SONG FOR A CHILD

My kitty has a little song
She hums inside of her;
She curls up by the kitchen fire
And then begins to purr.

It sounds just like she's winding up
A tiny clock she keeps
Inside her beautiful fur coat
To wake her, when she sleeps.

Helen Bayley Davis

MONTAGUE MICHAEL

Montague Michael
You're much too fat,
You wicked old, wily old,
Well-fed cat.

All night you sleep
On a cushion of silk,
And twice a day
I bring you milk.

And once in a while,
When you catch a mouse,
You're the proudest person
In all the house.

Anonymous

THE DANCING BEAR

Oh, it's fiddle-de-dum and fiddle-de-dee,
The dancing bear ran away with me;
For the organ-grinder he came to town
With a jolly old bear in a coat of brown.
And the funny old chap joined hands with me,
While I cut a caper and so did he.
Then 'twas fiddle-de-dum and fiddle-de-dee,
I looked at him, and he winked at me,
And I whispered a word in his shaggy ear,
And I said, "I will go with you, my dear."

The dancing bear he smiled and said,
Well, he didn't say much, but he nodded his head,
As the organ-grinder began to play
"Over the hills and far away."
With a fiddle-de-dum and a fiddle-de-dee;
Oh, I looked at him and he winked at me,
And my heart was light and the day was fair,
And away I went with the dancing bear.

Oh, 'tis fiddle-de-dum and fiddle-de-dee,
The dancing bear came back with me;
For the sugar-plum trees were stripped and bare,
And we couldn't find cookies anywhere.
And the solemn old fellow he sighed and said,
Well, he didn't say much, but he shook his head,
While I looked at him and he blinked at me
Till I shed a tear and so did he;
And both of us thought of our supper that lay
Over the hills and far away.
Then the dancing bear he took my hand,
And we hurried away through the twilight land;
And 'twas fiddle-de-dum and fiddle-de-dee
When the dancing bear came back with me.

Albert Bigelow Paine

MONKEY

WHEN YOU TALK TO A MONKEY

When you talk to a monkey
      He seems very wise.
He scratches his head
      And he blinks both his eyes;
But he won't say a word.
      He just swings on a rail
And makes a big question mark
      Out of his tail.

Rowena Bennett

BROTHERS

That handsome little chimpanzee
Looks very much like you—or me!

William Cole

MONKEYS ON THE BED

Three little monkeys
Jumping on the bed;
One fell off
And knocked his head.
Momma called the doctor,
The doctor said:
"No more monkeys
Jumping on the bed."

Anonymous

MOUSE

LITTLE MISS LIMBERKIN

Little Miss Limberkin,
   Dreadful to say,
Found a mouse in the cupboard
   Sleeping away.
Little Miss Limberkin
   Gave such a scream,
She frightened the little mouse
   Out of its dream.

Mary Mapes Dodge

THE OLD WOMAN

You know that old woman
   Who lived in a shoe?
She had so many children
   She didn't know what to do?

I think if she lived in
   A little shoe-house
That little old lady was
   Surely a mouse!

Beatrix Potter

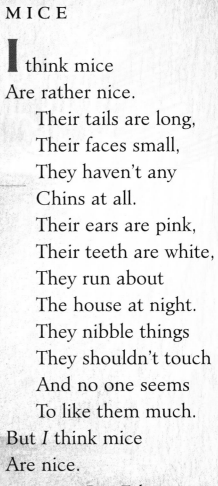

MICE

I think mice
Are rather nice.
　　Their tails are long,
　　Their faces small,
　　They haven't any
　　Chins at all.
　　Their ears are pink,
　　Their teeth are white,
　　They run about
　　The house at night.
　　They nibble things
　　They shouldn't touch
　　And no one seems
　　To like them much.
But *I* think mice
Are nice.

Rose Fyleman

SEA GULL

THE SEA GULL

I watched the pretty, white sea gull
Come riding into town;
The waves came up when he came up,
Went down when he went down.

Leroy F. Jackson

■ 14 ■

DUCK

THE PRAYER OF THE LITTLE DUCKS

Dear God,
give us a flood of water.
Let it rain tomorrow and always.
Give us plenty of little slugs
and other luscious things to eat.
Protect all folk who quack
and everyone who knows how to swim.

Amen

Carmen Bernos de Gasztold

THE DUCK

Behold the duck.
It does not cluck.
A cluck it lacks.
It quacks.
It is specially fond
Of a puddle or pond.
When it dines or sups,
It bottoms ups.

Ogden Nash

THE HAIRY DOG

My dog's so furry I've not seen
His face for years and years:
His eyes are buried out of sight,
I only guess his ears.

When people ask me for his breed,
I do not know or care:
He has the beauty of them all
Hidden beneath his hair.

Herbert Asquith

OLD SAGER

Took old Sager out a-huntin' one night,
    Blind as he could be;
He treed eleven possums up a sour gum stump,
    I'll be danged if Sager can't see.

Anonymous

TOM'S LITTLE DOG

Tom told his dog called Tim to beg,
And up at once he sat,
His two clear amber eyes fixed fast,
His haunches on his mat.

Tom poised a lump of sugar on
His nose; then, "Trust!" says he;
Stiff as a guardsman sat his Tim;
Never a hair stirred he.

"Paid for!" says Tom; and in a trice
Up jerked that moist black nose;
A snap of teeth, a crunch, a munch,
And down the sugar goes!

Walter de la Mare

DOGS

I had a little dog,
    and my dog was very small.
He licked me in the face,
    and he answered to my call.
Of all the treasures that were mine,
    I loved him best of all.

Frances Cornford

■ 17 ■

DANCE A JIG

Come dance a jig
To my granny's pig,
    With a raudy, rowdy, dowdy;
Come dance a jig
To my granny's pig,
    And pussy-cat shall crowdy.

Anonymous

I HAD A LITTLE PIG

I had a little pig,
I fed him in a trough,
He got so fat
His tail dropped off.
So I got me a hammer,
And I got me a nail,
And I made my little pig
A brand-new tail.

Anonymous

RABBIT

THE RABBIT

When they said the time to hide was mine,
I hid back under a thick grape vine.

And while I was still for the time to pass,
A little gray thing came out of the grass.

He hopped his way through the melon bed
And sat down close by a cabbage head.

He sat down close where I could see,
And his big still eyes looked hard at me,

His big eyes bursting out of the rim,
And I looked back very hard at him.

Elizabeth Madox Roberts

FROG

GRANDFATHER FROG

Fat green frog sits by the pond,
Big frog, bull frog, grandfather frog.
Croak-croak-croak.
Shuts his eye, opens his eye,
Rolls his eye, winks his eye,
Waiting for
A little fat fly.
Croak, croak.
I go walking down by the pond,
I want to see the big green frog,
I want to stare right into his eye,
Rolling, winking, funny old eye.
But oh! he hears me coming by.
Croak-croak—
SPLASH!!

Louise Seaman Bechtel

THE POLLIWOG

Oh, the Polliwog is woggling
In his pleasant native bog
With his beady eyes a-goggling
Through the underwater fog
And his busy tail a-joggling
And his eager head agog—
Just a happy little frogling
Who is bound to be a Frog!

Arthur Guiterman

■ 20 ■

TURTLE

THE LITTLE TURTLE

There was a little turtle.
He lived in a box.
He swam in a puddle.
He climbed on the rocks.

He snapped at a mosquito.
He snapped at a flea.
He snapped at a minnow.
And he snapped at me.

He caught the mosquito.
He caught the flea.
He caught the minnow.
But he didn't catch me.

Vachel Lindsay

THE PUM NA-NA FROGS

Pum na-na,"
say the frogs
on a rainy season night
when the moon is bright.

"Pum, pum, pum-na-na,
pum, pum pum-na-na."
They sit in their muddy pools
thinking
that candleflies
are shooting stars.

John Lyons

THE LION

The Lion, the Lion, he dwells in the waste,
He has a big head and a very small waist;
But his shoulders are stark, and his jaws they are grim,
And a good little child will not play with him.

Hilaire Belloc

ALLIGATOR

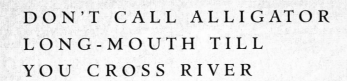

DON'T CALL ALLIGATOR
LONG-MOUTH TILL
YOU CROSS RIVER

Call alligator long-mouth
Call alligator saw-mouth
Call alligator pushy-mouth
Call alligator scissors-mouth
Call alligator raggedy-mouth
Call alligator bumpy-bum
Call alligator all dem rude word
but better wait

       till you cross river.

John Agard

BIRD

CATCH HIM, CROW!

Catch him, crow! Carry him, Kate!
Take him away till the apples are ripe;
When they are ripe and ready to fall,
Here comes baby, apples and all!

Anonymous

A LITTLE COCK SPARROW

A little cock sparrow sat on a green tree,
And he chirruped, he chirruped, so merry was he.
A naughty boy came with his wee bow and arrow,
Says he, I will shoot this little cock sparrow.
His body will make me a nice little stew,
And his giblets will make me a little pie too.
Oh, no, said the sparrow, I won't make a stew,
So he clapped his wings and away he flew.

Anonymous

■ 24 ■

MRS. PECK-PIGEON

Mrs. Peck-Pigeon
Is picking for bread,
Bob-bob-bob
Goes her little round head.
Tame as a pussy cat
In the street,
Step-step-step
Go her little red feet.
With her little red feet
And her little round head,
Mrs. Peck-Pigeon
Goes picking for bread.

Eleanor Farjeon

THE SECRET

We have a secret, just we three,
The robin, and I, and the sweet cherry-tree;
The bird told the tree, and the tree told me,
And nobody knows it but just us three.

But of course the robin knows it best,
Because he built the—I shan't tell the rest;
And laid the four little—something in it—
I'm afraid I shall tell it every minute.

But if the tree and the robin don't peep,
I'll try my best the secret to keep;
Though I know when the little birds fly about
Then the whole secret will be out.

Anonymous

SEA LIFE

THE SEA

Behold the wonders of the mighty deep,
Where crabs and lobsters learn to creep,
And little fishes learn to swim,
And clumsy sailors tumble in.

Anonymous

SALAMANDER

SAMUEL

I found this salamander
Near the pond in the woods.
Samuel, I called him—
Samuel, Samuel.
Right away I loved him.
He loved me too, I think.
Samuel, I called him—
Samuel, Samuel.

I took him home in a coffee can,
And at night
He slept in my bed.
In the morning
I took him to school.

He died very quietly during spelling.

Sometimes I think
I should have left him
Near the pond in the woods.
Samuel, I called him—
Samuel, Samuel.

Bobbi Katz

JIM-JAM PYJAMAS

He wears striped jim-jam pyjamas,
You never saw jim-jams like those,
A fine-fitting, stretchy, fur cat-suit,
Skin-tight from his head to his toes.

He wears striped jim-jam pyjamas,
Black and yellow and dashingly gay;
He makes certain that everyone sees them
By keeping them on all the day.

He wears striped jim-jam pyjamas,
He walks with a smug-pussy stride;
There's no hiding his pride in his jim-jams
With their zig-zaggy lines down each side.

He wears striped jim-jam pyjamas
And pauses at times to display
The effect as he flexes his torso—
Then he fancies he hears people say:

"I wish I had jim-jam pyjamas!
I wish I were feline and slim!
Oh, look at that brave Bengal tiger!
Oh, how I should love to be him!"

Gina Wilson

THE DONKEY

I saw a donkey
　　One day old,
His head was too big
　　For his neck to hold;
His legs were shaky
　　And long and loose,
They rocked and staggered
　　And weren't much use.
He tried to gambol
　　And frisk a bit,
But he wasn't quite sure
　　Of the trick of it.
His queer little coat
　　Was soft and grey
And curled at his neck
　　In a lovely way.

His face was wistful
　　And left no doubt
That he felt life needed
　　Some thinking out.
So he blundered round
　　In venturous quest,
And then lay flat
　　On the ground to rest.
He looked so little
　　And weak and slim,
I prayed the world
　　Might be good to him.

Gertrude Hind

HORSE

RIDING TO MARKET

Ride a cock-horse to Coventry Cross,
 To see what Emma can buy;
A penny white cake I'll buy for her sake,
 And a twopenny apple pie.

Anonymous

I HAD A LITTLE HORSE

I had a little horse,
 His name was Dapple Gray,
His head was made of gingerbread,
 His tail was made of hay.
He could amble, he could trot,
 He could carry the mustard pot.

Anonymous

ELEPHANT

OLIPHAUNT

Grey as a mouse,
Big as a house,
Nose like a snake,
I make the earth shake,
As I tramp through the grass;
Trees crack as I pass.
With horns in my mouth
I walk in the South,
Flapping big ears.
Beyond count of years
I stump round and round,
Never lie on the ground,
Not even to die.
Oliphaunt am I,
Biggest of all,
Huge, old, and tall.
If ever you'd met me,
You wouldn't forget me.
If you never do,
You won't think I'm true;
But old Oliphaunt am I,
And I never lie.

J.R.R. Tolkien

I ASKED MY MOTHER

I asked my mother for fifty cents
To see the elephant jump the fence.
He jumped so high that he touched the sky
And never came back till the Fourth of July.

Anonymous

L A M B

from SPRING

Little lamb,
Here I am;
Come and lick
My white neck;
Let me pull
Your soft wool;
Let me kiss
Your soft face;
Merrily, merrily, we welcome in the year.

William Blake

BILLY GOAT

There was a young goat named Billy
Who was more than a little bit silly.
They sent him to school
But he just played the fool
And ate satchels and books willy-nilly.

Anonymous

BUTTERFLY

Climbing a steep hill
I saw below, on a tree's
top twig, a butterfly.

Kwaso

from TO A BUTTERFLY

I've watched you now a full half-hour,
Self-pois'd upon that yellow flower;
And, little Butterfly, indeed
I know not if you sleep or feed.

How motionless!—not frozen seas
More motionless; and then
What joy awaits you, when the breeze
Hath found you out among the trees,
And calls you forth again!

William Wordsworth

FIREFLY

Although the night is damp,
The little firefly ventures out,
And slowly lights his lamp.

Anonymous

from
FIREFLY

I think
if you flew
up to the sky
beside the moon,
you would
twinkle
like a star.

Li Po

Please don't go!" I called,
but the fireflies flashed away
deep into darkness.

Onitsura

KANGAROO

THE KANGAROO

Old Jumpety-Bumpety-Hop-and-Go-One
Was lying asleep on his side in the sun.
This old kangaroo, he was whisking the flies
(With his long glossy tail) from his ears and his eyes.
Jumpety-Bumpety-Hop-and-Go-One
Was lying asleep on his side in the sun,
Jumpety-Bumpety-Hop!

Anonymous

OSTRICH

HERE IS THE OSTRICH

Here is the ostrich straight and tall,
Nodding his head above us all.

Here is the long snake on the ground,
Wriggling on the stones around.

Here are the birds that fly so high,
Spreading their wings across the sky.

Here is the bushrat, furry and small,
Rolling himself into a ball.

Here is the spider scuttling round,
Treading so lightly on the ground.

Here are the children fast asleep,

And here at night the owls do peep.

Anonymous

Index